Ladybird would like to thank Jane Swift for additional illustration work.

Published by Ladybird Books Ltd
A Penguin Company
Penguin Books Ltd, 80 Strand, London WC2R 0RL, UK
Penguin Books Australia Ltd, Camberwell, Victoria, Australia
Penguin Books (NZ) Ltd, Cnr Airbourne and Rosedale Roads, Albany, Auckland, 1310, New Zealand

1 3 5 7 9 10 8 6 4 2

Printed in Italy

Busy Garage

written by Melanie Joyce
illustrated by Sue King

It's a very busy day at
Busy Garage.
Sam the mechanic is hard at work.
He taps and bangs underneath
a car.

Sid the apprentice passes Sam
his tools.
Those overalls won't be clean
for long!

Down the lane there's an odd noise.
Putt-putt-putt. Ker-chug-chug-chug.
Farmer Stan's on his old red tractor.
It doesn't seem to be running
too well.

In the yard it splutters to a halt.
Will Sam know what's wrong?

"Sounds like dirt in your diesel,"
says Sam.
"I'll get it fixed as quickly as
I can."

Sam fits a new filter.
He fiddles around.
Soon the engine runs without
any splutters.

"Thanks for your help, Sam," says
Farmer Stan.
He reverses the tractor into
the lane.
Suddenly there's a loud
BEEP-BEEP!

A little blue car comes round
the bend.
"Watch out, Farmer Stan,"
shouts Sam.
Guess what happens next?

The tractor stops.
The little car swerves.
It squeezes past.
Then it skids to a halt.

"Phew," that was close, says Stan with a gasp.
But who is driving the car?

It's Pam the postwoman.
Is she all right?
"I'm fine," says Pam, "I just got
a fright."

"My car felt funny. But I don't know why."
Will Sam know what's wrong?

"Looks like you've got a flat tyre,"
says Sam. "We'll put a new one
on. It won't take long."
But Pam isn't happy at all.

"If I have to wait, the post will be too late," sighs Pam, with a wrinkly frown.

But Farmer Stan has got a plan.
"I'll help deliver the post," he says.
"By the time it's done, your car
will be fixed! There's no need to
worry at all."

And off they go.

Sid brings the toolbox.
And Sam gets to work.
He takes off the wheel.
Then he fits a new tyre.

The job's nearly finished.
There's just one last thing.

"This car needs a wash," says
Sid with a nod.
He gets a sponge and some
special shampoo.

And he rubs and scrubs
and polishes.
Soon the car looks as good as new.
But what's that noise in the lane?

It's Farmer Stan and Postwoman
Pam.
They think the car looks as clean
as a whistle.

"Thank you everyone," says Pam.
And she gives them all a kiss.
That's nice, isn't it?

It has been a long day at
Busy Garage.
Sid the apprentice is very tired.
"I know what the problem is,"
says Sam.

"We just need to have a nice cup
of tea."
And they do!